HOCKEY NIGHT
IN KENYA

HOCKEY NIGHT IN KENYA

Danson Mutinda & Eric Walters

illustrated by
Claudia Dávila

orca Echoes

ORCA BOOK PUBLISHERS

Printed in Canada and the United States in 2020 by Orca Book Publishers.
orcabook.com

Library and Archives Canada Cataloguing in Publication
Title: Hockey night in Kenya / Danson Mutinda, Eric Walters ;
illustrated by Claudia Dávila.
Names: Mutinda, Danson, author. | Walters, Eric, 1957– author. |
Dávila, Claudia, illustrator.
Series: Orca echoes.
Description: Series statement: Orca echoes
Identifiers: Canadiana (print) 20200184660 | Canadiana (ebook) 20200184679 |
ISBN 9781459823617 (softcover) | ISBN 9781459823624 (PDF) | ISBN 9781459823631 (EPUB)
Classification: LCC PR9381.9.M86 H63 2020 | DDC j823/.92—dc23

Library of Congress Control Number: 2020931809

Summary: In this illustrated short chapter book, two Kenyan
orphans get to experience the joy of playing ice hockey.

Orca Book Publishers is committed to reducing the consumption of
nonrenewable resources in the making of our books. We make every
effort to use materials that support a sustainable future.

Orca Book Publishers gratefully acknowledges the support for its publishing
programs provided by the following agencies: the Government of Canada,
the Canada Council for the Arts and the Province of British Columbia
through the BC Arts Council and the Book Publishing Tax Credit.

Cover artwork and interior illustrations by Claudia Dávila

Printed and bound in Canada.

24 23 22 21 • 2 3 4 5

For Henry, a dear father and friend.

The Story Behind the Story

While the story about Kitoo and Nigosi is made up, there is a great deal of truth in it.

It takes place in the Republic of Kenya, a country that sits directly on the equator. This is perhaps one of the last countries in which you would expect ice hockey to exist. In 2005 in Kenya's capital, Nairobi, the first ice rink in all of East Africa opened at the Panari Sky Centre Hotel. Although the rink is small, measuring only 105 feet (32 meters) by 39 feet (12 meters), it is home to the Kenya Ice Lions, Kenya's only ice-hockey team. As of this writing, the team is made up of thirty players, most of whom began skating on rollerblades. The team is led by captain Ben Azegere, and their ultimate goal is going to the 2022 Olympics. The players recently traveled to Canada, a trip sponsored by Canadian coffee-and-donut chain Tim Hortons, and had an opportunity to play against and train with a team that included some NHL players.

The orphanage portrayed in the book is the Hope Development Centre, which was founded in 2007 by my parents, Henry and Ruth Kyatha, and Eric and Anita Walters. It's in a small community, Kikima, in the Mbooni district, which is about 68 miles (110 kilometers) from Nairobi. With the passing of my father,

I became the patron of the program. Eric was made an elder more than a decade ago and is an important member of the community.

As of this writing there are eighty children in the residence, another sixty-four in residence in high school, college or university, and another twenty-five who reside in the homes of extended family members. In addition, more than forty of our young people have graduated from college, university or trade school. These graduates include a banker, an IT specialist, teachers, researchers, auto mechanics, hospitality-industry members and hairdressers.

The orphanage described in the story is a beautiful big blue building that sits on the grounds of my family homestead, or shamba. This is the area where my ancestors have lived for thousands of years. The building and the children who reside there are right outside the front window of my home.

Members of the Kenyan hockey team visited our orphanage. During their visit, they played a three-hour game of floor hockey with the children in the dining hall. It was a great treat for the kids to engage in a sport that most of them had never heard of, let alone played. The team promised to visit again, and you can imagine how much the kids anticipate their next visit!

—Danson Mutinda

Chapter One

"The test is now finished," Mr. Mutinda said.

The students all put down their pencils. Kitoo had already completed all the questions and was checking his answers for the second time. Kitoo was a good student, and he took care with his work. He looked over at his best friend, Nigosi, and gave him a look as if to ask, *Did you do okay?*

Nigosi gave him a small smile and a thumbs-up. Kitoo was happy for his friend.

"Leave the tests on your desk as you depart for your lunch meal," Mr. Mutinda ordered.

The students got to their feet and picked up their packs and lunch containers. Kitoo, Nigosi and the other students who lived at the orphanage always had breakfast before they left in the morning and were given lunches to take. They were lucky—many of the children, even those who lived with parents or other relatives, hadn't eaten at all today and might not have a lunch. Having a parent didn't mean you didn't go hungry.

They filed out of the classroom, and the two boys headed over to the shade of the big tree where the fourth-grade students gathered. Kitoo and Nigosi always ate together, breakfast, lunch and dinner. They also shared a bunk bed,

Kitoo on the bottom, Nigosi on the top, in the little room they shared with fifteen other boys at the orphanage.

All the children were orphans who had lost both their mothers and fathers and didn't have anyone else to care for them.

Nigosi had been only a year old when his parents passed away, and he had then been cared for by his grandfather. His grandfather was a kind man, but he was very old, and he became too frail to care for his young grandson. Nigosi entered the orphanage at age six.

Kitoo's parents had died when he was only a baby. He'd been passed from one relative to another until finally he ended up on the streets by himself. There he had been found by staff and brought to the orphanage.

Kitoo remembered well that first day at the orphanage. He'd been so scared, but Nigosi had told him that he didn't need to be afraid. Kitoo had a family again, a very big family, and Nigosi was his new brother. And in many ways they *were* brothers.

They both pulled out their lunch containers. Kitoo had a bright blue plastic container, and Nigosi's was red.

Kitoo started to open the lid, then stopped. "I think we have pilau today."

The rice dish with onions, spices and pieces of meat was Kitoo's favorite food. Nigosi's too.

"We do not have pilau," Nigosi said.

"I can smell it," Kitoo said as he brought the container up close to his nose and inhaled deeply.

"You always think you can smell it, and you are always wrong."

"Maybe today I am right."

"Pilau is only on special days," Nigosi said.

"This is a special day. It is Tuesday, and I am sitting with my best friend. What could be more special than that?"

Nigosi laughed.

"What if the cook decided that today, as a surprise, we would all get pilau?" Kitoo asked.

"That *would* be a surprise," Nigosi admitted. "But I think it is githeri."

Githeri was a mix of corn and beans. It was what the children ate for lunch every day and often for supper as well.

Nigosi went to remove the lid of his container.

Kitoo stopped him. "Close your eyes and imagine for just a minute."

"It will not change what is in there," Nigosi said.

"Maybe not, but it will make you happy, at least for a while. Sometimes you have to dream."

Nigosi smiled. Kitoo was a dreamer. It was one of the things Nigosi liked about him. So Nigosi closed his eyes and inhaled deeply. Strangely, he almost thought he could smell pilau, and it did make him happy.

He opened his eyes, and Kitoo was looking at him.

"Did you smell the pilau?"

Nigosi nodded. "I did. I could smell it."

"Now we open our lunches."

They removed their lids at the same time.

"It is githeri!" Kitoo exclaimed. He sounded genuinely surprised. "Maybe tomorrow it will be pilau, but for now I am still happy."

"You are?"

"Of course. Githeri is my *second-*favorite meal."

Nigosi laughed.

Using their fingers, they each scooped up their lunch. Kitoo did like the githeri. It was tasty and filling. The orphanage had bags and bags of corn and bags and bags of beans in the supply room beside the kitchen. One of Kitoo's chores was to help keep this room tidy. He swept the floor and moved the bags so that the newest went to the back and the oldest food was eaten first. It made him happy to know there were always so many bags of food waiting to be mixed and eaten.

Once the boys had finished their meal, they walked over to the little water spout that came from the big tank. This tank and the four others that sat on the grounds of the school collected rainwater from the roofs of the school buildings. It was the middle of the dry season, and it hadn't rained for almost two months, so two of the tanks had already run dry.

Making sure not to use too much water, the boys carefully rinsed their containers clean and put them into their schoolbags.

Out in the schoolyard some of the other children were kicking a ball around. The yard was nothing more than bare red dirt, and as they chased the ball they kicked up clouds of dust behind them.

"Are you coming to play?" Nigosi asked, although he already knew the answer.

"No. I have to go and help Mrs. Kyatha."

Mrs. Kyatha was the teacher who ran their school library.

"You help her every lunch. You could come and play today."

"You play football every lunch. You could come and help in the library," Kitoo said.

"But you are very good! And you like playing football."

"I am even better at reading."

"Then you don't need to do it so much. Mrs. Kyatha would understand if you wanted to play today instead."

"She would understand, but she needs my help."

Nigosi shook his head. "I am going to play."

He put his pack down against the fence, ran out to the field and joined in the game. Kitoo headed for the library.

Chapter Two

Kitoo walked down the aisle and ran his fingers along the shelf. There were not nearly as many books as it would take to fill the tall wooden shelves. He knew all these books well, as he had read everything the little library held. Whenever he touched a favorite, he paused for a few seconds and smiled. Some he had read more than a dozen times. Kitoo wished there were more books, new books, books he hadn't read.

Mrs. Kyatha had told him there were almost as many books in the world as there were grains of sand on a beach by the ocean. He believed her, even though he'd never been to a beach or seen an ocean. In fact, Kitoo had never been farther than a short drive from his school and the orphanage where he lived, which were in the mountains of Kenya. Except when he was reading those books—through them he'd traveled around the world.

"Have you found a book you wish to read today?" Mrs. Kyatha asked.

He shrugged. "I was hoping to find something new."

"There is no money for new, but would you be willing to look at something old?"

She gestured for him to follow her. She sat down at the circulation desk and pulled out a box.

"I found these books in the back, in the storage room."

Kitoo peered into the box. There had to be at least two dozen books. They were dusty, and he could see that some were yellowed and the pages were curled at the corners.

"These are old books, and I must throw them away," Mrs. Kyatha said.

"Throw away books!" Kitoo exclaimed.

"Books not only give life, but they have a life," the librarian explained.

"But to throw them away?" Kitoo asked.

"I am not pleased either," she said. "Some were damaged when rainwater came through the roof a few years ago. Others are just so old and have been used so much that they are missing covers and have torn pages. I knew they needed to be discarded, but I could not bring myself to do it." She paused. "Then today I saw you and thought perhaps there is another solution."

He waited. What could that solution possibly be?

"I thought there might be a book or two you wish to have."

"Have? Do you mean *own*? The books would be mine?"

"I can think of no other person who would be a better owner. But, as I have told you, they are in very poor condition. Would you like to look?"

"Yes, ma'am. Please, ma'am."

Mrs. Kyatha pushed the box closer to Kitoo, and he started to go through it. The book on top was an old textbook missing its cover.

"You look while I help other students," the librarian said.

He pulled out the next few books, saddened when he realized that they were almost beyond saving. Those that had gotten wet when the water came through the roof during a long-gone rainy season were swollen and spongy. As Mrs. Kyatha had warned, many were missing covers. The pages of some were stuck together, and as he tried to open them, they ripped in his hands. Pages had been torn out of others. He couldn't imagine doing such a thing to a book! For him books were not just special, they were almost like living creatures.

But there was one book that looked promising. Like the others, it was yellowed and the pages had curled at the corners. But it had a cover, a cover with a title Kitoo loved—*Sports Around the World*.

He opened it and started flipping through the pages. A few of them were ripped and others stuck together, but most of the book seemed fine. He kept turning pages and came to a sport he knew. A sport he had played! There were pictures of men playing cricket in India. He looked up at the big map on the wall behind the librarian's desk and quickly found India. He knew where almost all the countries were on the map, as they had studied them in class.

Some more pages of the book were stuck together, so he turned to the next open one. It showed men in thick clothing. They wore helmets on their heads and gloves on their hands, and they were holding sticks. It looked like field hockey, but they had big boots on their feet. Under the picture it said *Ice Hockey,* and the country was Canada. That country was really easy to find—it was gigantic! It was colored pink and was near the top of the map. It looked like it was almost half as big as all of Africa. Kitoo wondered if that could even be possible.

Mrs. Kyatha walked over. "That is frozen water they are skating on," she explained as she stood beside him. "I imagine you have never seen ice."

He shook his head no.

"It is cold, like ice cream," she said.

Of course, he knew about ice cream, although he'd never tasted it.

"They are wearing ice skates," she said. "They have metal blades on the bottom. I have seen people playing ice hockey."

"You have?"

"I lived in Canada for many years when I was in university. It is very far away, and in the wintertime there is snow and ice everywhere!"

He couldn't even imagine that.

"I have also seen them play hockey in Machakos."

"They have ice in Machakos?" he exclaimed.

Mrs. Kyatha laughed. "Oh no, they were on pavement, and the skates had wheels, but they were still playing hockey. Have you ever been to Machakos?"

"Twice…no, three times," he said.

Machakos was a city that was a thirty-minute drive from their little town. Kitoo had gone there with the orphanage driver, Jackson, to help him pick up supplies. It was the farthest Kitoo had ever been from home. Machakos had many more buildings and people than Kikima, and almost all the roads were paved.

"It was at People's Park that they were playing," Mrs. Kyatha said.

"I have seen that park!"

Jackson and Kitoo had driven by it, and he had looked from the window of the truck through the fence of the park. There were rides for children and a lake with little boats, and there were tables where people sat and ate. He had seen all of that, but he hadn't seen anybody playing hockey.

"Have you been inside the park?" Mrs. Kyatha asked.

Now it was his turn to laugh. "I wish, but no. I have just seen it as we drove by."

"Perhaps someday you could go there and see the roller hockey players. Perhaps someday you could even play," Mrs. Kyatha said.

"Someday." Kitoo knew many things were possible but that most would never happen.

"Would you like to have this book?" Mrs. Kyatha asked.

"Yes, ma'am!"

"Are you sure it is not too damaged?"

"It is perfect!"

She laughed. "It is far from perfect, but it is now yours." She picked up the book and handed it to him. "Now you continue to look through the box. Perhaps there are others you wish to claim."

Chapter Three

"You need to put it away," Nigosi said.

Kitoo looked up from the book, *his* book, and smiled.

"We have to go now or he will go without us, and you will only ever see pictures."

Kitoo closed the book. He carefully put it away with his other two books in the locker at the foot of his bed. Each child in the orphanage had the same big blue metal locker where they kept all the things that were personal to them.

In Kitoo's locker he had his clothes—his good going-to-church clothing, his school uniform and his play clothing. There were two pairs of shoes, one dress-up pair and a pair that he used for play. His sandals were waiting at the door. He had two broken metal toy cars and the three books that he now owned thanks to Mrs. Kyatha.

One was a book about farming, another was about rocks and, of course, there was the one about sports. Of all the sports, the one of most interest to him was ice hockey. It was because of this book that he was going for a drive today.

Kitoo closed the lid of the locker and put the little lock in place. He put the key in his pocket and rushed to catch up with Nigosi. He slipped on his sandals and ran to the truck. The engine was already running, the driver, Jackson, at the wheel and Nigosi sitting up front at his side. Kitoo climbed in beside his friend, happy that he'd have the window.

Almost immediately Jackson started to drive. They bumped out of the orphanage courtyard, up the hill and onto the road leading to town. The truck left behind a trail of dust as they drove.

"Thank you for letting us come with you today," Kitoo said.

"Thank you for offering to help," Jackson replied.

The boys were going to help, but that wasn't the only reason they had come along.

Kitoo looked out the window as Nigosi asked Jackson questions about driving. Nigosi hoped that when he

grew up he could also become a "pilot" —a driver, like Jackson.

Jackson was kind to all the children at the orphanage, but Nigosi was one of his favorites. Nigosi helped him clean the truck and was always there to watch as Jackson changed tires or the oil or fixed the engine. Jackson was a good mechanic and was also handy at fixing things around the orphanage. Recently he had been showing Nigosi how to do little jobs here and there.

Kitoo wasn't interested in being a pilot, but he understood why his friend was. It was wonderful to watch the world as it sped by. It was wonderful to be in control of such a powerful machine and to be able to travel. In a truck like this they could go to Machakos, where they were headed today, or even to Nairobi.

"Are you ready?" Jackson asked Nigosi.

"Yes, sir, I'm ready!"

Nigosi put his hand on the gear shift that came up from the floor of the truck in front of him.

"Now put it in fourth gear!" Jackson said.

He depressed the clutch, and Nigosi put the truck into the next gear. There was a slight jerk and then, as Jackson released the clutch, the truck surged forward.

"Very good! Well done!" Jackson said. Nigosi looked so happy, so proud.

The roads were rough, with holes and bumps. At times they had to slow down to get around a large rock or a particularly big hole.

Along the way they passed other trucks and dozens and dozens of little motorbikes. Most of the bikes carried big bags of goods as well as a passenger. Some were carrying more than one passenger.

Up ahead, coming toward them on the road, was a yellow matatu. Jackson didn't slow down, but he steered the vehicle to the very edge of the road to give the bus room. The brightly painted bus barreled past them. Its roof was piled high with boxes and barrels, and there were even a few people sitting up there. One of the women on the roof waved to them as the bus roared past, barely missing them.

"Those matatus act like they own the road," Nigosi said.

"They are bigger than other vehicles, and a good driver must give them space. You will be a good driver someday," Jackson said.

"I will try."

"Perhaps when I am too old to drive, you will be the driver for the orphanage," Jackson said.

Nigosi again looked very proud.

The road underneath them changed from dirt to pavement, a sign that they were nearing the city. More and more people were walking along the roadside, and there were now many more vehicles around them. Up ahead Kitoo could see the tall buildings. Soon the road was lined with stores, and there was so much traffic that they had to slow down.

Jackson eased the truck through the traffic and bumped over the curb and into the parking lot of the market. Here they were going to get the supplies they needed for the orphanage. He drove around to the back of the building, where other trucks were loading supplies as well.

"You boys stay with the truck, and I will go inside and arrange for our order," Jackson said.

He left and went into the store. The boys climbed out and waited at the side of the truck.

"This city is very exciting," Kitoo said.

"It is nothing compared to Nairobi," Nigosi said. "You have never been to Nairobi, have you?"

"I have been there the same way you have been to Canada. I have read about it."

There were books about Nairobi, the capital of Kenya, in the library.

Mrs. Kyatha also had an old booklet about Canada, and Kitoo read it often.

She had shared stories about living there. She had told him about the winters with the snow and ice and how on Saturday nights it seemed like the whole country sat by their televisions and watched hockey. Kitoo knew a great deal about Canada.

Jackson returned from the building. He had a receipt in his hand. "I have purchased eighty bags of corn and forty bags of beans. Now the work begins."

Chapter Four

It had taken them almost two hours to load the truck. The bags were so heavy that it took both Kitoo and Nigosi to move one at a time, and even then it was only with help from Jackson that they were able to lift them into the truck. Kitoo could feel the strain in his arms.

Loaded down with the extra weight, the truck was moving much slower now. Jackson eased it through the narrow streets, past vehicles and people, and pulled into the parking lot of the Tea Tot restaurant. It was well-known for having the best samosas in the whole area, and Jackson had offered to buy some for Kitoo and Nigosi to thank them for their work. The boys had a different idea.

Jackson turned off the engine. "Are you boys sure you do not wish to have samosas?" he asked.

Nigosi looked at Kitoo to answer. "We are grateful for the offer," Kitoo said.

"And we *do* want samosas," Nigosi added. "But we will gratefully take the shillings."

Jackson handed them each a ten-shilling note. That was enough for two samosas, but it was also enough for admission to the People's Park.

"You can find your way to the park?" Jackson asked.

"Yes, sir," Nigosi said. "A good pilot knows how not to get lost."

"Then I will eat and talk to my friends. You boys need to be back at the truck in one hour."

"We will, sir," Kitoo said.

Jackson went into the restaurant, and the two boys hurried toward the park. The streets were filled with people and lined with stores. Many of the stores had music blaring out of their open doors.

"How do people live with so many others?" Kitoo asked.

"It is crowded, but I could like this," his friend said. "Maybe someday I will live in Nairobi."

They crossed the street, careful of the trucks and cars and aware of the little motorbikes that flitted through the crowd. Soon they came to the tall metal fence of the park. Behind it they could

see the rides. A tall, circular ride called a Ferris wheel stood out.

"Can you imagine how exciting it would be to ride on that?" Nigosi said.

"I think we would need more shillings. But it would be amazing."

"As those samosas would be too," Nigosi said.

"You can go back if you wish."

Nigosi shook his head. "You are my friend. This is more important to you, so it is more important to me."

They walked up to the entrance gate. Two security guards were taking money for admission. They were both big men, wearing uniforms and outfitted with clubs. Kitoo felt nervous.

"Have you boys come to go on the rides?" one guard asked.

"No, sir," Nigosi said. "But we do have money for admission."

"But not for the rides?" the other security guard asked.

"No, sir," Kitoo said. Both boys held out their shillings. "We have come to see the roller hockey players."

One guard looked at the other. "What do you think?"

"If they are not going to ride, well…"

"Keep your shillings. Go and watch. The skaters are on a paved path by the lake," he said, pointing in that direction.

The boys rushed through the gate and toward the lake. There were people everywhere, mostly children with their parents. They were eating treats and were all dressed better than the two boys were.

They passed by the rides. Some spun around, others went high, and some looked like little cars and trucks. And each ride had a line of children waiting to get on.

"There they are!" Nigosi yelled.

Kitoo looked. He could see the players racing around. He and Nigosi ran to get closer. There were ten or eleven players, all holding hockey sticks. They wore helmets on their heads, and some had pads on their legs and gloves on their hands. They looked very much like the players in the pictures in Kitoo's book, except that they were on rollerblades and were chasing an orange ball instead of a black puck.

The players flew by, moving quickly. They turned and swooped, and some of them even skated backward. They hit the orange ball with their sticks, and it flew into the air and across the rink. Then they all turned and chased it.

There were five men sitting on a wooden bench at the side. When players got tired, they were replaced by others who had been resting on the bench. The men took turns playing, skating as fast as they could after the orange ball.

"They are so fast!" Nigosi said.

"And so skilled," Kitoo added. "Can you imagine being able to do that?"

"You can imagine playing. I can only imagine watching."

Nigosi took a seat on the ground, and Kitoo sat beside him. This was exactly what he'd hoped to see, and it was happening right before his eyes. It was amazing.

Chapter Five

"We have to go," Nigosi said as he got to his feet.

"What?" Kitoo asked. He'd been staring so hard at the players that he hadn't heard his friend.

"It is time. We need to get back to Jackson."

"Perhaps we could stay a few minutes more," Kitoo said.

"No. We need to leave." Nigosi offered his friend a hand and helped him to his feet. "We must leave now."

Kitoo reluctantly nodded.

They started to walk away, but Kitoo kept looking back, not wanting to go, wanting to watch the skaters just a little bit longer. He was not watching where he was walking, and he bumped straight into a trash bin. He looked down into the bin and could hardly believe his eyes. There amid the trash was a rollerblade!

He reached in and picked it up. The skate was missing two wheels. There was a second boot beneath the first one. It was missing all of its wheels, and the whole undercarriage was gone. It was just a plastic boot.

Kitoo held them up for Nigosi to see.

"Hey!" a loud voice called out.

Kitoo turned around. One of the players was yelling at the boys. He waved his stick in the air and then skated down the pavement toward them.

"Put them back in the trash bin," Nigosi urged his friend.

Before Kitoo could react, the man was in front of the boys, towering over them. Kitoo felt afraid, but the man smiled.

"You were watching us play," he said.

"Yes, sir," Kitoo answered. "We came from Kikima to watch you."

"I have been to the market there. Kikima is not close. I see you have taken that pair of broken skates."

"I meant no harm. I can put them back in the bin."

"No need, but they are badly broken. They need a few wheels, and one needs a new carriage. Perhaps my friends and I can be of assistance."

———

They bumped along the way home. The boys hadn't kept Jackson waiting— he had been enjoying his time with his friends in the restaurant. What *was* waiting were three samosas for each boy! They were so good! Almost as good as pilau. Kitoo was going to pretend that his next lunch was samosas instead of pilau.

The boys had offered to give back the shilling notes they hadn't needed to enter the park, but Jackson had said to keep them.

So Kitoo had a ten-shilling note in his pocket and assorted rollerblade pieces on his lap. Along with the two boots he had taken from the trash bin were some things given to him by the players. He had six extra wheels. Three were chipped, but the other three were almost new. And he had been given another old set of boots. Both toes were smashed, and the wheels were gone, but the undercarriages were intact. Perhaps with a little help he could take all the pieces that didn't work and create one pair that did.

"Jackson," Nigosi said, "you are so good at fixing the truck when it is broken."

"I do what needs to be done," Jackson said.

"And you can fix cars too?" Nigosi asked.

"Cars, trucks, motorcycles—all of them," Jackson said.

"It sounds as if you could fix anything with wheels," Nigosi said.

Kitoo now knew what his friend was getting at.

Obviously, Jackson did as well. "I imagine I could fix rollerblades too," he said. "When we get home, I will get my tools, and we shall see."

Chapter Six

Kitoo rolled around the dining hall. It was the only paved surface at the orphanage. In fact, it was the only paved surface in all of Kikima.

In his hands was a field-hockey stick that his teacher, Mr. Mutinda, had given him. Kitoo had fashioned a ball out of plastic and twine, and he pushed it forward as he rolled around tables and chairs. He had been skating for almost two months now and hardly ever fell anymore.

Jackson had been able to take all the pieces Kitoo had collected and assemble two working skates. They were different colors and sizes, with the right skate being much bigger, but Kitoo made do by shoving rags in that toe. Jackson had also shown Kitoo how to change the wheels and oil the bearings to make sure they rolled smoothly.

There were almost a dozen younger orphans sitting off to the side, watching Kitoo skate. He almost always had an audience. Watching him was like nothing else they had ever seen.

Kitoo made a tight turn, and they cheered. He spun around and started to skate backward, and they cheered even louder. He smiled to himself. He was showing off a little because it was nice to have an audience.

Kitoo could skate forward and backward, turn, spin around and stop.

It had been very difficult, and he had had to use a table or chair to keep himself from tumbling over. He had fallen down many times—more times than he could count. At first it had seemed like he would never be able to skate like the hockey players in the park, but with practice he had gotten better.

Of course, he had school to attend and homework to complete, as well as many chores to do around the grounds of the orphanage, but he skated whenever he could find the time.

Sarah, the matron, and James, the cook, weren't happy at first with Kitoo using the dining room, but Kitoo had always been helpful to them, just as he was with everybody. Now sometimes he would skate around and carry plates, containers and food from the kitchen to the tables in the dining hall. He was practicing *and* helping!

"You will not shoot it past me this time!" Nigosi yelled. He stood with a broom in his hand, in front of a table that had been turned on its side to act as the net. He had old socks over his hands to protect them from the ball.

Kitoo skated faster. He lifted up his stick and struck the ball. It sailed up past Nigosi's outstretched hand and hit the top corner of the table.

"Goal!" Kitoo shouted.

"You arc a vcry good hockey player," Nigosi said. "I think you are the best hockey player in all of Mbooni!"

"I am the only hockey player in Mbooni."

"I think you would be one of the best players in Machakos too," Nigosi said.

Kitoo laughed. "It would be wonderful to play with the others."

"Do you think they would let you play?" Nigosi asked.

"They were kind. Perhaps they would allow me to play someday."

"I will ask Jackson if we can go with him when he picks up supplies next month. We could help load the truck, and then I would watch and you would play."

Kitoo slumped beside his friend and leaned against the makeshift net. He pulled the small booklet Mrs. Kyatha had given him out of his pocket and showed it to his friend.

"The best ice-hockey players are in Canada," Kitoo said. "There is so much cold there that people even live in houses made of ice."

"No, that cannot be."

"I will show you." Kitoo flipped through the pages until he came to a picture. "They are called igloos."

"Ice houses. No wonder they are such good ice-hockey players. They can skate inside their own homes!"

Kitoo laughed. He turned to another page. "And their police officers dress all in red, and they ride horses." He showed Nigosi another picture.

"And do the horses wear skates as well?" Nigosi asked.

"That would be funny. The police have cars as well, and they must use them in the wintertime," Kitoo said. "You know, if I lived there I could skate on ice instead of on this concrete floor."

"Someday that could happen," Nigosi said.

Kitoo shook his head. "Canada is very far away."

"It is not the only country in the world that has ice."

"The countries that do are *all* very far away," Kitoo said.

"Perhaps you could rollerblade all the way to one of those countries."

"If only it were that simple. I will never skate on ice."

"You disappoint me," Nigosi said.

Kitoo was surprised.

"Aren't you the boy who dreams at each lunchtime that there will be pilau instead of githeri?" Nigosi asked.

"Yes, but aren't you the boy who thinks I am a dreamer for thinking that?"

"Yes, so now you need to dream more. The next time you are about to enter the dining hall, I want you to stop and think that there will be ice where the concrete is."

"Even I cannot dream that much."

"It will happen. Someday you will skate on ice. I am certain," Nigosi said.

"How can you be so certain?"

Nigosi smiled. "I just am. I just am. Do you smell it?"

"Smell what?" Kitoo asked.

"Pilau." Nigosi took a deep breath. "They are making pilau for dinner."

"They are making githeri," Kitoo said. Earlier, with his skates on, he had helped the cook by carrying in bags of corn and beans for their evening meal.

"Close your eyes," Nigosi said.

Kitoo looked at his friend, whose eyes were already closed.

Kitoo closed his eyes too.

"Well?" Nigosi asked.

"Yes, I think I can smell it," Kitoo said.

"Good. Now you must believe that in some way, someday soon, you will see ice," Nigosi said.

"Pilau, I have seen. Ice, I have never seen."

"Sometimes you just need enough faith," Nigosi said. "I am certain that someday you will see ice. Maybe sometime sooner than you think."

Nigosi got to his feet. "Now you should get up and try to score again."

He offered his friend a hand and pulled Kitoo onto his skates.

"But there will be a difference now," Nigosi said. "This time I will stop you!"

Kitoo laughed. "And you think I am a dreamer!"

He skated off, pushing the ball with his stick.

Kitoo knew he might never get to see ice. He knew he might never have pilau for lunch or even for dinner ever again. But he also knew what a good friend he had in Nigosi.

Chapter Seven

Jackson gave a little toot of the horn to let the boys know he was ready to go. They ran to the truck. Kitoo carried a bag that contained his rollerblades and some pads that the matron, Sarah, had made out of rags to put over his shins. They weren't quite like the pads the men had been wearing, but they would give him some protection. Nigosi carried his friend's field-hockey stick. It wasn't the same as an ice-hockey stick, but it was all he had.

They climbed into the truck, and Jackson drove toward the gate of the orphanage. Sarah came running out of the main building. She was carrying something and waved for the truck to stop. She reached through the window and handed the boys two sweaters.

"These are for you," she said. "I do not wish for you to get cold."

Kitoo was confused. It was a hot day.

"Um, I believe it is going to get cold before you are home. The night air can be damp," Sarah said.

Kitoo was even more confused now. They would be home before night, unless they were getting more supplies than he thought.

"And Kitoo, I want you to take great care and not get hurt. Do you understand?"

"I will be careful," Kitoo replied.

The adults at the orphanage had agreed that after Kitoo and Nigosi had helped load the supplies, there would be time for Kitoo to go and skate at the park. And maybe he would even be able to play roller hockey. It made him happy to think this could possibly happen.

Jackson put the truck back in gear, and they were off again. They went through the gate, up the long hill of the driveway and onto the road.

"Thank you for coming to help," Jackson said. "I have one stop to make in Kikima."

Jackson pulled into the little fuel station at the top of the hill on the edge of the town. He got out to arrange for the vehicle to be filled with gas. It was a market day, so the station was very busy with people coming to town to stock up on goods. Still, the busyness of Kikima was nothing compared to Machakos.

"Good morning!" someone sang out.

It was Mrs. Kyatha.

"Good morning," they all responded.

"You boys need to move over," she said as she pulled open the door. They shuffled over on the seat, and she climbed in.

"I have arranged to come with you," she said. "I am going to the city.

Maybe I could even watch you play hockey."

"How do you know I am going to play hockey?"

"Um, I see your stick—and isn't that the bag in which you carry your rollerblades?" she asked.

Of course that was it! Everybody in the town seemed to know how much he loved playing.

Jackson finished fueling the truck and climbed back in, and they were off again.

"Thank you for allowing me on your journey," Mrs. Kyatha said to Jackson.

"It is good to have you along, my cousin."

"Boys, my father is the brother of Jackson's mother," she explained.

It was not surprising that they were related. Most of the people in the village were related to many others. Even the children who were orphans and needed to go to the orphanage often had many cousins in the community.

As Jackson drove they passed many other vehicles. With a quick glance he could tell the make and model of each one and the year it was made. Nigosi would ask him questions about the engine size of a vehicle, or how much weight it could carry, or how many passengers. Jackson seemed to know every answer, and Nigosi listened intently. Kitoo knew his friend would be a good driver someday.

Time passed quickly on the drive, and soon they came to the outskirts of Machakos. Coming into the city was always exciting for the boys, but today, for Kitoo, it was even more exciting.

Jackson drove toward the supply store—and then right past it. Kitoo thought they must be going to a different store today. People's Park came up beside them. Through the fence Kitoo could see people strolling around the grounds. In the distance he saw the Ferris wheel. He had a plan involving that ride.

He had brought along the ten-shilling note he had saved on the last trip. If Jackson offered them a few more shillings for their help, he was going to use it to purchase a ticket for Nigosi to ride the Ferris wheel. It made him smile to think of his friend being so high in the sky.

But they didn't stop there. They kept driving, and the park disappeared behind them. Soon there were fewer stores and less traffic and less people. It seemed like they had left the city behind.

"Where are we going?" Kitoo asked.

"To the store."

"But we are no longer in Machakos."

"The store is in Nairobi," Jackson said.

"Nairobi!" Kitoo exclaimed.

"Sometimes I travel to Nairobi for supplies."

"That is exciting, but…" Kitoo let his sentence trail off.

"But you had wanted to play hockey at People's Park in Machakos," Jackson said.

Kitoo nodded.

"That is not the only place where hockey is played in Kenya," Mrs. Kyatha said. "There is a place in Nairobi where *many* people play hockey, and we will go there instead."

Kitoo still felt concerned. He had hoped to see the kind man who had helped him with the rollerblades and parts, or some of his friends. He had wanted to show them how well he could skate. He had also hoped they might be willing to allow him to play with them.

"Don't look so disappointed," Nigosi said. "It will be wonderful in Nairobi!"

Kitoo looked at his friend. "How do you know that?" he asked.

"I'm just sure," Nigosi said. "How could it not be so?"

Chapter Eight

Kitoo sat on the edge of his seat, leaning forward, staring through the windshield of the truck. He had heard about Nairobi, but nothing had prepared him for what he was seeing. There were so many people, more than he could count, and they were everywhere! There were six lanes of traffic, three in each direction, and every lane was so filled with cars and trucks and buses that they were all just inching forward. The road was lined on both sides with stores and shops and factories. And then there were the buildings. He hadn't thought any could be taller than those in Machakos, but now he knew he was wrong. Some here were so high that they reached up into the sky.

"Isn't it amazing?" Nigosi asked.

"I can hardly believe my eyes," Kitoo said.

"I told you that someday we would see Nairobi."

"Yes, but you also said someday I would see ice."

Both Jackson and Mrs. Kyatha laughed.

Jackson turned off the main road and went down a driveway. Kitoo looked up. They were driving toward a tall glass tower. It didn't look like a store. Then he saw the lettering over the entrance— *The Panari Hotel*. Why would they come here?

Jackson brought the truck to a stop at the front door of the building. Around them, fancy cars were parked in the long curving driveway.

"You should get out here, Kitoo, and you need to take your skates and stick," Jackson said.

"But it is a hotel," Kitoo replied.

"It is also a place where people skate."

Mrs. Kyatha climbed out of the truck, and the boys followed closely behind. Kitoo took his things, and Nigosi helped by carrying his stick.

"I am going to pick up supplies," Jackson said through the still-open door. "I will be back in a few hours."

"Shouldn't we help?" Kitoo asked.

"You have other things to do."

Mrs. Kyatha closed the door of the truck, and Jackson drove away.

A man in a fancy uniform was standing by the big glass front doors of the hotel. Mrs. Kyatha approached and spoke to the man in Kikamba, the language spoken by all the people in Kikima, and he replied in the same language. Kitoo figured the man must be from their tribe. She asked about skating, and he pointed and gave directions. They *were* playing hockey here. The man opened the door and gestured for them to go inside. The boys stayed close to Mrs. Kyatha as they entered the hotel.

The lobby was very fancy, with carpets and big furniture and many people, all dressed nicely. Kitoo felt like people were looking at them. He and Nigosi were dressed so differently, and Nigosi was the only person holding a field-hockey stick.

A man stood up from a chair in the lobby. He was wearing a tracksuit that was green, black and red, the colors of the Kenyan flag, and he was holding a small bag and a hockey stick. He came toward them.

"Ah, you must be Mrs. Kyatha," he said.

"And you are Mr. Mohammed," she replied.

The two shook hands.

"Mr. Mohammed is the manager of the hockey team," she explained to the boys.

"Am I to assume that this young man holding the stick is the person who will be joining us today?"

"Oh no!" Nigosi said. "I am only holding it." He handed the stick to Kitoo.

"This is Kitoo. He will be playing. He is very good," Mrs. Kyatha said.

"The very best," Nigosi said.

Mr. Mohammed smiled. "We shall soon see if that is true. Come. Follow me."

They walked through the lobby, down a hallway and through a set of metal doors. It led them to a large open room. There was no furniture except for a wooden bench on one side of the room. There was no carpet on the cement floor. The metal doors closed loudly behind them.

"Put on your skates," Mr. Mohammed said. He motioned to the bench at the side of the room.

Kitoo hesitated, and Nigosi took him by the arm and led him to the bench.

"Why are there no other players?" Kitoo whispered.

"He wants to see if you are as skilled a player as we said," Nigosi whispered back.

"I have old broken skates that do not match or even fit."

"They fit well enough," Nigosi said.

"I have a field-hockey stick."

"You do well with the stick you have. You are the best in Kikima, and now you will show him you are the best in Nairobi."

"But what if I am not?"

"Maybe you are not the best, but you are still very good," Nigosi said. "Can I tell you something?"

Kitoo nodded.

"I think I can smell pilau."

———

Kitoo got to his feet and took a few steps. The floor felt very smooth under his wheels. Much smoother than the floor of their dining hall. He did a couple of quick little turns.

Mr. Mohammed called to him, and he skated over.

"We need to trade sticks."

Mr. Mohammed took the field-hockey stick and gave him a real hockey stick.

Kitoo looked down at it. It was just like the ones that the men in People's

Park used. It was just like the ones used by real ice-hockey players!

Mr. Mohammed pulled an orange ball from a bag and dropped it to the floor in front of them.

"Now let's see what you can do!"

Kitoo had never even held a real hockey stick before. He had never used a real ball before. He had never been on a floor so large and smooth and open. Was he really good, or was he just an orphan boy from Kikima skating on broken blades that had been thrown away? There was only one way to find out.

He started skating, pushing the ball along in front of him with his stick. This ball rolled much more evenly than the one he had fashioned out of plastic and twine.

Kitoo spun around and started skating backward. He was able to use this real stick, with a bigger blade and a longer shaft, to keep the ball right in front of him.

He spun back around so he was skating faster and faster. He pulled the stick back and hit the ball as hard as he could, and the ball flew up into the air and hit the wall with a loud *bang*!

"Stop skating!" Mr. Mohammed yelled.

Kitoo looked over and slowed down.

"I have seen enough."

Kitoo put his head down and skated back to Mr. Mohammed. If he had just had a little more time, he could have shown him more.

"You need to take off the skates," Mr. Mohammed said.

"I am sorry," Kitoo said. He felt so bad.

"Sorry?" Mr. Mohammed asked. "Sorry for what?"

"For not being better."

Mr. Mohammed laughed. "You are very good."

"But why do you wish me to stop?" Kitoo asked.

"I want you to stop because it is time to start something different. Something better."

Chapter Nine

A little shudder went up Kitoo's spine. He wasn't sure if it was because he was cold or because he was scared. Maybe it was both. He knew he would be much colder if he wasn't wearing the heavy sweater that Sarah had sent with them. In front of them was a long white sheet of ice. It was hard to believe that such a thing existed except in books or in places like Canada, but here it was, in Nairobi. Mr. Mohammed had told them it was the only ice rink in all of East Africa.

Kitoo exhaled, and his breath came out like smoke.

"It is like we are on fire," Nigosi said as he exhaled. "Although I do not know how fire can live in such cold."

"It is cold. We should thank our matron for giving us our heavy sweaters," Kitoo said.

"I told you that you would see ice," Nigosi said.

"You knew of this plan and did not tell me?" Kitoo asked.

"It was to be a surprise. You are surprised, right?"

"I could not be more surprised if I had been given wings."

"You have wings—when you skate, you fly!" Nigosi replied.

"This is different," Kitoo said as he gestured to his feet. "These skates have no wheels."

"Wheels or metal, it does not matter. Skating is skating. You will be great."

"We shall see," Kitoo said.

"I know you will do well."

"How do you know?" Kitoo asked.

"I am *very* smart," Nigosi said. "Now just think of the ice."

Out on the rink half a dozen people were skating around. They wore proper hockey equipment and had helmets on. Kitoo was wearing a similar helmet to protect his head, and the pads he'd been given for his legs. The skaters were all much older than Kitoo. They were men, and he was a boy. There were dozens of pucks on the ice, and the men were shooting them at a net and passing them between each other. All the while they were skating very fast.

Mr. Mohammed came over. "Kitoo, they told me your dream is to play ice hockey."

"Yes, sir."

"I have a dream too. I dream that one day Kenya will be known not just for its distance runners but also for its hockey players. Is that dream too big?"

Kitoo thought before he spoke. "Sir, I was an orphan living on the streets. Now I live in a fine building with my own bed. I go to school, and I eat every day. I have a family. I am here in ice skates, getting ready to step onto the ice in Nairobi. How could any dream be too big?"

Mr. Mohammed laughed. "Maybe you could be part of my dream. Someday you might be one of my hockey players, but now it is time to stop dreaming and start doing."

"Yes, sir."

Kitoo stood up. He wobbled back and forth on the thin metal blades and braced himself with his hockey stick. He shuffled forward a few feet, and Mr. Mohammed opened the gate.

"It will be different, but it will be the same. Do you know what to do when you fall?" Mr. Mohammed asked.

"I will get back up."

He gave the boy a pat on the back.

Kitoo put one foot onto the ice, and his blade almost scooted out from under him. He held onto the boards with one hand and held his stick with the other as he took a second step. He was on ice!

He pushed off with one foot and glided forward. He was skating. He did it again and again and again. He was ice skating!

In front of him was a puck. He reached out with his stick, lost his balance and fell to the ice with a thud. The ice was hard and cold. He felt the cold through his sweater. He knew what he had to do. The same thing he did when he fell the first time that he tried to roller-skate. He would get up.

Kitoo rose to one knee and then got to his feet. He almost lost his balance again. He pushed off and started skating. With the blade of the stick he pushed the puck forward. It slid along the ice, and he caught up to it. He moved his legs, pushing off and gliding, left and right, going faster and faster. The puck stayed on his stick as he made a turn. It was the same as being on rollerblades.

It was hard. It was different, but he just knew he could do it. He turned, crossing his blades over each other the same way he did with his rollerblades.

In front of him, guarding a net, was a goalie. He was wearing heavy pads, and his helmet had a metal screen to protect his face. Kitoo had never shot a real puck before. He had never taken a shot on anybody, except Nigosi holding a broom. What would it be like to shoot at a real goalie? Could he score the way he scored on his friend? There was only one way to know.

Kitoo pushed the puck forward. He pumped his legs harder, pushing hard and gaining speed. He came closer and closer. He pulled back his stick and hit the puck. It shot along the ice and skidded into the corner of the net. He had scored! He had scored!

Kitoo turned around. Mrs. Kyatha, Nigosi and Mr. Mohammed were all cheering. He couldn't stop himself from smiling.

One of the players skated to his side. "Nice goal. Are you ready to play?"

"If I could?"

"It is time. It is hockey night in Kenya."

Danson Mutinda's parents, Ruth and Henry Kyatha, cofounded the Hope Development Centre orphanage with Eric and Anita Walters in 2007. When Henry passed away, Danson became patron of the program. He and his coauthor, Eric Walters, worked together to write this story of two energetic and joyful children who are based on many of the children they work with at the centre. He lives in Kikima, Kenya, on the grounds of the orphanage.

Eric Walters is a Member of the Order of Canada and the author of over 115 books that have collectively won more than 100 awards, including the Governor General's Literary Award for *The King of Jam Sandwiches*. A former teacher, Eric began writing as a way to get his fifth-grade students interested in reading and writing. Eric is a tireless presenter, speaking to over 100,000 students per year in schools across the country. He lives in Guelph, Ontario.

To find out more about the Kenyan hockey team or to make a donation to help them with their dream of going to the Olympics, please go to kefis.co.ke/press.

If you wish to know more about our children's program or make a donation to the Hope Development Centre, please visit hopestory.ca/where-we-work/kenya.